Dear Parents and Educators,

Welcome to Penguin Young Readers! As parents and educators, you know that each child develops at their own pace—in terms of speech, critical thinking, and, of course, reading. Penguin Young Readers recognizes this fact. As a result, each Penguin Young Readers book is assigned a traditional easy-to-read level (1–4) as well as an F&P Text Level (A–P). Both of these systems will help you choose the right book for your child. Please refer to the back of each book for specific leveling information. Penguin Young Readers features esteemed authors and illustrators, stories about favorite characters, fascinating nonfiction, and more!

The Little Engine's Easter Egg Hunt

LEVEL **2**

F&P TEXT
LEVEL **I**

This book is perfect for a **Progressing Reader** who:
- can figure out unknown words by using picture and context clues;
- can recognize beginning, middle, and ending sounds;
- can make and confirm predictions about what will happen in the text; and
- can distinguish between fiction and nonfiction.

Here are some **activities** you can do during and after reading this book:
- Read the Pictures: Use the pictures in this book to tell the story. Have the child go through the book, retelling the story just by looking at the pictures.
- Make Connections: The Little Engine works with all her friends to solve the clown's riddles. Have you ever solved a problem with friends? How did you work together?

Remember, sharing the love of reading with a child is the best gift you can give!

*This book has been officially leveled by using the F&P Text Level Gradient™ leveling system.

To Alexander and Noah, my little engines.
Love you the most!—LE

For AJ—JH

PENGUIN YOUNG READERS
An Imprint of Penguin Random House LLC, New York

Penguin supports copyright. Copyright fuels creativity, encourages diverse voices,
promotes free speech, and creates a vibrant culture. Thank you for buying an authorized
edition of this book and for complying with copyright laws by not reproducing, scanning,
or distributing any part of it in any form without permission. You are supporting
writers and allowing Penguin to continue to publish books for every reader.

Copyright © 2020 by Penguin Random House LLC.
Based on the book THE LITTLE ENGINE THAT COULD (The Complete, Original Edition)
by Watty Piper, illustrated by George & Doris Hauman, © Penguin Random House LLC.
The Little Engine That Could®, I Think I Can®, and all related titles, logos, and characters are
trademarks of Penguin Random House LLC. All rights reserved. Published by Penguin Young Readers,
an imprint of Penguin Random House LLC, New York. Manufactured in China.

Visit us online at www.penguinrandomhouse.com.

Library of Congress Cataloging-in-Publication Data is available upon request.

ISBN 9780593094341 (paperback)   10 9 8 7 6 5 4 3 2 1
ISBN 9780593094358 (hardcover)   10 9 8 7 6 5 4 3 2 1

The Little Engine That Could®

The Little Engine's Easter Egg Hunt

by Lana Edelman
illustrated by Jannie Ho

The Little Engine chugs
along happily.

4

Spring is here, and today is Easter!

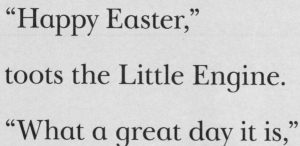

"Happy Easter,"
toots the Little Engine.

"What a great day it is,"
says the toy clown.

"Are you ready to
have some fun?"

The toy clown has a surprise
for his friends.
"It is time for an Easter
egg hunt!" he says.

Everyone cheers.

"There are chocolate eggs

hidden somewhere on the hill,"

the toy clown says.

"You can use these baskets

to collect them."

"But how will we know

where to look?"

asks the Little Engine.

"That is where the fun begins!"

the toy clown says.

"Here is your first clue."

"From net to net we like to run.

We pass and kick,

and have some fun!"

reads the Little Engine.

The Little Engine looks at the clue.

She reads it again.

This is going to be

harder than she thought.

"I can help you," says the girl doll.

"Yeah, we can all help you!"

adds the giraffe.

The Little Engine toots

with excitement.

"I know! The soccer field!"

shouts the monkey.

The Little Engine leads the way.

Puff, puff, chug, chug!

They look high.

They look low.

But . . .

There are no chocolate eggs here.

"But look—another clue!" shouts the boy doll.

"To keep you safe, we work so hard, with ladders and hoses from the yard," reads the monkey.

"The firefighters at the firehouse!"

shouts the giraffe.

Puff, puff, chug, chug!

They look high.

They look low.

But . . .

There are no chocolate eggs here.

"But look—another clue!"

says the monkey.

"All day long we love to play.

We moo and baa the day away!"

reads the giraffe.

"The farm!" says the girl doll.

Puff, puff, chug, chug!

They look high.

They look low.

But . . .

There are no chocolate eggs here.

The Little Engine hangs her head.

Will they ever find

their chocolate eggs?

"We can't give up now!"
says the girl doll.

"We've gotten this far
by working together.

If we keep it up, I know we will find
our chocolate eggs!" she says.

"I think we can, I think we can!"

the Little Engine cheers.

They look high.

They look low.

And . . .

"Around the bunny's tail!"

shouts the monkey.

"You have worked together to find the clues, so follow us in two by twos!" reads the boy doll.

The bunnies hop away.

"Let's follow them!"

says the Little Engine.

They come to a field.

And . . .

It's the Easter Bunny!

"Welcome to our Easter party!"

shouts the toy clown.

"We did it!"

cheers the Little Engine.

Happy Easter

31

The Little Engine celebrates
with chocolate eggs, bunnies,
and the best friends she could
ask for.